A Friend for Mr. Granville

by **Gillian Richardson**

illustrated by
Claudette MacLean

Copyright © 1997 by Gillian Richardson

We acknowedge the support of the Canada Council for the Arts and the Alberta Foundation for the Arts for our publishing program. Thanks to Kim Smith of Priority Printing. A special thanks to Glen Huser who edited all four Hodgepogs and produced the teacher's guides.

Editor: Glen Huser
Production Editor: Peggie Graham
Original book design: Gerry Dotto
Cover art and interior illustrations: Claudette MacLean
Page set-up and interior design: Chao Yu
In-house co-ordination: Mary Woodbury

A Hodgepog Book for Kids

Published in Canada by Hodgepog Books, an imprint of The Books Collective, 214-21, 10405 Jasper Ave, Edmonton, Alberta, Canada T5J 3S2. Telephone (403)448-0590

Canadian Cataloguing in Publication Data

Richardson, Gillian
    A Friend for Mr. Granville

ISBN 1-895836-38-7

I. MacLean, Claudette
PS8585. I193F74 1997   jC813'.54   C97-910640-0
PZ7.R3944Fr 1997

In loving memory of my dad
who loved the sea.

Chapter 1

"I wish we didn't have to go back again," Trevor complained.

"Twice more," Logan said from his seat one row over in the classroom. "Once to take these pictures, and later to cook stuff. I wish we could skip the pictures. I'd rather eat."

Trevor sighed. "Me too. This is a dumb picture." He scrunched up his paper. "I'd rather draw nuclear subs."

"You've never seen a nuclear sub, Trevor Milton." Kristie said as she walked past his desk.

"Have so! Lots of times. On TV. So there." Trevor tried to grab Kristie's paper but she was too quick.

Anna looked up from her picture of a log cabin. "Ms. Gilbert said you had to use your ears and your imagination. You should have listened better to the stories those old people told us."

"Pooh. They were boring," Trevor said. "Who wants to know about old pioneer stuff anyway? What are you drawing, Logan?"

"A hay wagon. With horses. That white-haired man with the cane told us about growing up on the farm. He always got to ride on the wagon." Logan began to colour his picture.

"Well, I can't think of anything to draw," Trevor moaned. He tossed his crumpled paper across the aisle at Anna.

"Trevor! Put that in the garbage can, please." Ms. Gilbert had looked up from her desk at the wrong moment. "You may have one more piece of paper. Do some thinking before you start to draw this time."

Anna and Kristie giggled as Trevor shuffled over to the paper cupboard. When he returned to his desk, they were still talking about that morning's visit to the senior citizens' home.

"Did you know that tiny lady in the wheel chair is 97 years old? That's almost 100!" Kristie said in amazement.

"My grandma is 71. She tells me lots of stories," Anna said.

"I've got two grandmothers," Logan announced. "How many have you got, Trevor?"

"None," Trevor muttered, scowling at the blank

paper on his desk. "And my grandpa died last month. He was a sailor in the war. He used to tell me all about the submarines he saw." Trevor felt that sad, lonely feeling again. His mom told him she knew what it was like too. They both missed Grandpa.

"I hope we get to sit with Mrs. Murphy next week," Kristie said, adding two more birds to her picture. "She told us about when she went to school. They only had one classroom. Once there was a storm and they had to stay at school for three days!"

"Did you see that old man sitting by the window, all by himself?" Logan asked. "He didn't talk to anyone."

Trevor picked up his pencil. He **had** wondered about the man. "Yeah. He just stared out the window the whole time we were there."

"Maybe he doesn't like kids," Anna offered. "We have a neighbour like that. She gets real crabby if you even step on her lawn."

"My grandpa used to sit at the window like that sometimes," Trevor said, as he started to draw. "When he did that, my mom said he was remembering. He missed the sea."

"Maybe that old man was just lonely," Kristie suggested. "Next time, I'll go over and say hello."

"Let's both do it," Anna said. "We can show him our pictures too."

Logan leaned over to see what Trevor was doing. "You're supposed to draw pioneer stuff, Stupid. That's a submarine."

"I know what it is," Trevor said, grinning. "It's a memory. Like my grandpa had. Maybe that old man was thinking about the sea too. I'm drawing what he might have been thinking."

Logan shook his head and walked away. "I bet Ms. Gilbert won't go for that. Uh-uh. No way."

Trevor shrugged. He remembered how his drawings had often got his grandpa started on a story. Perhaps the old man had stories to tell too. He probably just needed someone to listen. Trevor decided he could do that job.

His mom had called it his 'special assignment', after Grandpa came to live with them. When everyone else was too busy, Trevor spent the time with

Grandpa. He never minded. It was fun listening, and he got to share the things that happened at school. But since Grandpa was gone, Trevor had lots of empty time.

For a final touch, he added a small flag with a maple leaf on it to the hull of his submarine. Maybe he'd show it to the old man by the window. He couldn't seem to stop thinking about him.

Chapter 2

Excited voices filled the bus as it stopped in front of the seniors' home the following week. Each child had brought artwork to show. Ms. Gilbert led them to some chairs at the front of the big room. The old people sat around on sofas and in wheel chairs.

"Sit here," Logan said, grabbing Trevor's arm. "It's close to the food table. Look at that chocolate cake. Yum!"

"Watch it, Logan," Trevor growled. "You're scrunching my picture." He'd managed to get out of having to do a real pioneer drawing, but now he felt funny. What if everyone laughed at him? The other kids were going to show log cabins, old schoolhouses, or families making candles.

Logan jabbed him in the ribs with his elbow. "Look, Trevor. He's still there." He pointed over to the window.

But Trevor had already noticed the silent old man who reminded him of his grandpa. This man looked older, the way he was bent forward in his chair. His wrinkled hands rested on his lap. He didn't seem to hear the children, or anybody else. He still stared out the window.

"What's wrong with him?" Logan whispered.

"He's old, that's all I guess," Trevor answered.

"Everyone here is old, but they don't sit and stare like that," Logan argued.

Kristie turned around in her seat and shushed him. Trevor looked out of the corner of his eye. Ms. Gilbert was watching them. He tried to listen to the other children telling about their pictures, but his eyes kept moving back to the old man. Finally, it was his turn.

"I drew a nuclear submarine," Trevor began, then was scared to go on.

Some of the kids giggled, but one lady said, "It's lovely, dear. Do you like submarines?"

Trevor nodded. "It's a memory, like the ones you told about, only it's a memory of the sea. It was because of my grandpa." There was silence in the room. Trevor felt his face getting red. Then he blurted out, "I thought he might be thinking about the sea too." He pointed to the old man.

Everyone in the room turned to look. "Oh, you mean Mr. Granville?" asked old Mrs. Murphy. "Did you draw your picture for Mr. Granville?"

Trevor nodded again.

"What a nice thought, dear," said Mrs. Murphy. "He doesn't talk, but you could show it to him. He'd like that I'm sure."

"Thank you, Trevor. You may sit down," Ms. Gilbert said. "We have three more pictures to see. April, you're next, please."

Trevor found his place beside Logan. He didn't pay attention to the rest of the presentations. He really wanted to talk to Mr. Granville. It was hard to sit still.

At last, Ms. Gilbert said, "Now children. the residents have invited us to share some treats with them. You may line up over by the table."

"Great! Let's go," Logan said, jumping up from his seat.

"In a minute." Trevor wanted to go by himself to give his picture to Mr. Granville. Maybe the old man would talk to him if he was alone.

"All the chocolate cake will be gone," Logan warned.

Trevor didn't listen. He walked quietly over to stand in front of the man's wheel chair.

"Hi." His voice came out squeaky. He cleared his throat and started again. "Hi. I'm Trevor Milton. I drew this for you." He held the picture up in front of Mr. Granville.

The old man lifted his head a little but didn't take his eyes from the window. He didn't say anything. Trevor began to feel embarrassed.

"It's a submarine. My grandpa was a sailor."

Mr. Granville sat unmoving.

Suddenly Kristie and Anna were standing beside Trevor. Kristie pushed in front of him, knocking the paper out of his hand.

"See mine? This is the old schoolhouse where Mrs. Murphy went to school. Do you like kids?"

Trevor backed away slowly. He kept looking at Mr. Granville, who still had not moved or spoken. The two girls kept talking, asking him all kinds of questions.

"Stop it, Kristie. Don't keep bugging him," Trevor shouted. "Leave him alone. He doesn't want to talk to you. Leave him alone." And he stomped off, leaving his picture of the submarine on the floor.

Chapter 3

Trevor stayed mad at Kristie all week. And he was mad that Mr. Granville had not looked at his picture. But he decided that had been Kristie's fault. If she and Anna hadn't barged in, he was sure Mr. Granville would have talked to him.

It was time for the class to make one last visit to the seniors' home. This time, the residents were going to teach them how to make some pioneer food.

"We're going to make blueberry jam," Kristie bragged to the others, as they boarded the school bus.

Trevor scowled. His name was on the same list as Kristie's. He wondered if Ms. Gilbert would let him switch to another group.

"We have to make SOURdough!" Logan groaned. "Sounds gross. I wish we could make chocolate cake, like we had last week."

12

Mr. Granville was pointing out the window. His head was moving too, and he seemed to be trying to lean forward in his chair.

Trevor looked quickly around. No one else had noticed. But why would they? Everyone was too busy and Mr. Granville had made no sound.

Trevor began to worry that the old man would fall out of his chair. What should he do? Something outside the window was getting Mr. Granville all excited. Trevor had to know what it was. He decided to go over and see what the old man was looking at. He glanced quickly along the table. No one was watching. Tim was trying to pour his sugar back into the bag so he could start measuring all over again. Trevor put down his cup and slipped away.

He came up behind the wheelchair so Mr. Granville wouldn't see him. He stood on tiptoe to see over the man's shoulder. Outside, on the lawn, were three people and a puppy. There was a small girl, younger than Trevor, a lady who was probably the girl's mother, and an older lady. Trevor had seen the second lady here in the seniors' home. She must be the grandmother, he thought. But it was the puppy that Mr. Granville seemed excited about.

The black and white puppy was small and quick. Mr. Granville followed every move. He turned his head as the puppy ran this way and that. From beside the wheelchair now, Trevor could see the old man was smiling. He decided to push the chair closer to the window.

"Trevor, what are you doing?"

Trevor jumped. He hadn't heard Ms. Gilbert come up behind him. He looked up at her, feeling shy.

"He never moved before," Trevor explained. "He always just sat and stared, even when I showed him my picture. He's watching the puppy. I thought he might want to get closer."

"Yes, I see. Perhaps it reminds him of his family. He certainly seems to be enjoying their fun," Ms. Gilbert said gently. "Do you want to stay here and keep Mr. Granville company instead of cooking, Trevor?"

Trevor nodded and smiled. That was exactly what he wanted. He stood with his hand on the arm of Mr. Granville's chair. The old man nodded and grinned, now and then pointing with a shaky finger at the small dog tearing around outside.

But as soon as the people left with the dog, Mr. Granville settled back in his chair. Before his hands fell back into his lap, he reached over and lightly touched Trevor's arm. Then his face went blank again. It was almost as if nothing had happened.

Trevor had forgotten what was going on in the room behind him. He began to tell Mr. Granville parts of his favourite stories. It felt like the times that he and his grandpa had spent together, except now Trevor was doing all the talking.

"Trevor? Here. I brought you one."

The voice was quiet, and Trevor looked up in surprise. It was Kristie, holding out a biscuit smothered with butter and dripping with blueberry jam.

Trevor felt better now. He wasn't even mad at Kristie anymore. He took the biscuit. "Thanks," he said.

"Why are you over here? You missed the cooking."

"I know. It's okay. I wanted to keep him company instead."

"But he doesn't talk."

"Yes, he does. In a way," Trevor said. He could still feel the feather-like brush of Mr. Granville's hand on his arm. "Anyway, it doesn't matter."

"What do you mean?" Kristie asked.

Trevor shrugged and took a big mouthful of biscuit so he wouldn't have to answer. It was hard to explain that seeing Mr. Granville feel happy had made him feel good too. And the old man had almost spoken to him, he was sure of it. He wished he could get to know Mr. Granville better. He wished Mr. Granville could have his own dog. Maybe they could play with it together. It would be almost like having a grandpa again.

Chapter 4

"I bet the grownups won't let you," Logan said, sitting cross-legged under a tree in Trevor's yard.

"Why not? It's a super idea. You didn't see how excited Mr. Granville got," Trevor answered. "Even the grownups want him to be happy, you know."

"But, Trevor, where would you get a puppy?" Kristie asked. "They cost money. Nobody would just give you one."

"I'm telling you, it'll never work," Logan said.

"Quit being such a pain, Logan. You said Ms. Gilbert wouldn't let me show my picture either and she did."

Logan tore out a handful of grass and tossed it at Trevor. "We've finished going there," he said.

"Anyway, the best part was the chocolate cake. I bet

there wouldn't be any more of that unless the whole class went back."

Trevor gave Logan his most disgusted look. He had hoped his friends would want to help with his plan. He wasn't sure it would work unless they all helped.

"Do you have any money, Trevor?" Kristie asked.

"Yeah. I've saved some of my allowance. But it's not very much." He stopped and looked at each of them. "We would all have to find jobs to do. Maybe we could collect bottles, or do some extra chores."

"That's dumb," Logan interrupted. "It's too much work."

"Maybe we could have a bake sale, or put on a circus," Kristie suggested.

"A circus! You're nuts. Where are you going to get the elephant and the tigers? It wouldn't be much of a circus without them," Logan sneered. "A bake sale might be okay. We could eat the leftovers."

Kristie stuck her tongue out at Logan.

"Are you going to help or just complain?" Trevor said to Logan. "A circus is too hard, Kristie. We need easy stuff, so we can get lots of money."

"But where are we going to find a puppy?" Kristie demanded again.

"We'll go to the Humane Society," Trevor said. "They have all kinds of dogs. And they don't cost much."

"Then why do we need so much money?" asked Kristie.

"Because, Dummy, the dog isn't the only thing we need."

20

"That's right, Kristie," Anna said. "We'll need a leash. And a bowl for food. And a bed for it to sleep in, and..."

"Hold it," Trevor hollered. It was his plan. He wanted the others to help, not take over.

"You've forgotten the most important thing," Logan said, rolling over on his back.

Trevor sighed. Logan was his best friend, but he sure was being difficult. "What? What do you think is so important?"

"The grownups. They won't let a puppy live in the seniors' home."

"Why not?"

"Who's going to clean up after it when it pees on the floor? Or poops? Who's going to take it for a walk? Who gets to pay for its food and stuff? What if it gets sick? What about..."

"Okay! Okay!" Trevor shouted angrily. "You sound just like a grownup."

"Yeah. Like my mom. It's exactly what she said when I asked for a dog. Parents hate dogs," Logan muttered.

Trevor was silent. What if Logan was right? He'd figured out where to find a dog, even some ways to pay for it. But the toughest job of all might be getting the people at the seniors' home to agree.

"Well, we have to try, that's all. You didn't see how much fun Mr. Granville was having. I bet he would talk too. He needs a puppy, and I'm going to get him one, whether you guys help or not." Trevor finished out of breath. He glared at Logan, but Logan stuck a blade of grass between his teeth and looked away.

No one spoke for a few minutes. Then Anna said, "We could talk to Ms. Gilbert. She's really interested in those old people, you know. It was her idea to take us there in the first place. Maybe she'd go back with us and talk to them."

Trevor stopped scowling. "Yeah! And maybe she could help us think how to find enough money."

"This might be fun," Kristie said, "even without a circus."

"You know, maybe a puppy isn't such a good idea," Anna started to say.

"Annnn-aah!" Trevor and Kristie both shouted at once.

"No, no. I don't mean the whole idea isn't a good idea. I mean, a puppy."

"Why not?" Trevor demanded.

"It's what Logan said. About cleaning up after it. We should get a dog that's all grown up. All trained. That would be one less problem, wouldn't it?" Anna looked around at the others.

"I guess so," Trevor agreed. "But it would have to be a small sort of dog too. One that could sit on Mr. Granville's lap."

"So we'd better look for a lap-dog," Kristie giggled. "All right?"

Anna nodded. Trevor smiled now too. "All right!" At least the girls were willing to help. He'd have to work on Logan.

Chapter 5

"It's a wonderful idea, Trevor!" Ms. Gilbert said when they told her about it the next day. "Do you think the three of you could manage it?"

"Four of us maybe," Trevor said, still thinking of ways to get Logan interested.

"You could ask the class if they'd like to help," Ms. Gilbert suggested. "But there could be an even bigger problem."

"What?" Kristie asked.

"I don't know what the Director of the home will say. Or the rest of the residents. You'd have to find out first if they want a dog."

"My dad says pets are good for old people. So they don't get lonely," Trevor added, pleased that he had an answer for that argument all ready.

"I can see why," Ms. Gilbert said, and laughed. "My cat talks to me all the time. But pets make work too. Older people might find that hard."

"We'll get one that's all trained," Kristie said quickly.

"And quiet," Anna put in before Ms. Gilbert could answer.

"We want to try anyway," Trevor told the teacher.

Ms. Gilbert looked at their hopeful faces. "Tell you what," she said. "Suppose we go back to the seniors' home and talk to the Director about this. Would you like me to arrange it?"

Trevor grinned and nodded. But his heart pounded. What would he have to say to make the Director agree? So far he hadn't even been able to talk his best friend into going along with the idea.

As he sat in the Director's office a few days later, Trevor kept rubbing his sweaty hands over the knees of his jeans. He looked around to see if the others felt nervous too.

Anna was trying to smooth a wrinkle from her shirt. Kristie twisted a strand of hair. Logan was there too, swinging his legs back and forth in a big chair. He hadn't promised to help, but today his parents had to go out of town so he was staying at Trevor's house.

"Well now, children. Sorry to keep you waiting." Mrs. Spencer, the Director, hurried in. She was a large lady. She made Trevor feel too small. "I understand you have an idea that our residents might enjoy?"

Ms. Gilbert looked at Trevor. "Go ahead," she encouraged.

Trevor swallowed hard. He wished he could have a big drink of water.

"It's about getting a dog. It would really be for Mr. Granville, but everybody could share it. We'd like to get him a dog."

"Mr. Granville?" Mrs. Spencer was puzzled.

Trevor fidgeted while Ms. Gilbert explained how Trevor had noticed the old man watching the puppy.

"I see," Mrs. Spencer said, raising her eyebrows.

"He needs a dog," Trevor said starting to feel braver. "He doesn't talk to anyone, so he must be lonely. The only time he moved was when he saw the dog outside. A dog would keep him company."

"Mr. Granville is very sad because his family is all gone," Mrs. Spencer explained gently. "He never says a word."

"But he might if he had a dog," Kristie said. "He could hug it, and talk to it."

"A small one," Anna added quietly. She looked at Trevor.

Trevor smiled his thanks weakly. He didn't think Mrs. Spencer seemed very interested in their idea.

"One that wouldn't pee on the floor." Kristie whispered, when no one else spoke.

Trevor saw Logan roll his eyes and smirk. He also saw the adults smile at each other. "We'd pay for everything," he offered quickly, before they could think of any problems.

"I've read about this sort of thing," Ms. Gilbert said, when the children had run out of things to say. "I understand many doctors like the idea of a pet to cheer up old people."

"That's true," Mrs. Spencer agreed.

Trevor began to hope.

"It is done in many homes. We haven't had any pets here because no one has asked for one. But I suppose if they wanted one..."

"Hurrah!" Kristie yelled.

"Not yet, Kristie," Trevor hollered, embarrassed.

Both adults laughed.

"It's a bit soon to celebrate, children," Mrs. Spencer said. "I didn't agree just yet. I'll have to ask the residents first. It would be mostly up to them, since it would be their pet."

"Perhaps the children would like to write a letter to explain their idea. We could come back when everyone has had time to think about it," Ms. Gilbert suggested.

"That's a good plan. Is that what you'd like to do?" the Director asked Trevor.

It wasn't really what Trevor wanted to do. But he nodded. "Okay," he agreed without looking at others.

"Good. Why don't you say hello to Mr. Granville again, before you leave? He'll be in the lounge." Mrs. Spencer said, standing up and holding out her hand to Trevor.

He wiped his own down his pant leg once more, then shook hands with her. He had hoped she would say yes right away. But at least she hadn't said no!

While Ms. Gilbert and the others stopped to talk to Mrs. Murphy, Trevor slipped away to where Mr. Granville sat, as usual; by the window.

"Hi," he said, shyly.

At first there was no response. Trevor wondered if Mr. Granville was sleeping, even though his eyes were open.

"Would you like to have a dog?" Trevor asked, keeping his voice low.

The old man gave a deep sigh, but otherwise didn't move. Trevor tried once more.

"We have a plan," he began, then he heard Ms. Gilbert calling him. They were ready to leave. "I'll tell you another time, okay?" Quickly, before the others came over, he patted Mr. Granville's arm and whispered, "See you soon."

To his surprise, the old man lifted his hand and clutched Trevor's sleeve. His head moved slightly.

It was all Trevor needed. "Bye. But don't worry. I'll be back," he promised.

Chapter 6

"I sure hope that letter works," Trevor said, as he walked home from school with Logan, Anna and Kristie.

"It's probably a waste of time," Logan moaned. "How come Ms. Gilbert made me stay anyway? I never said I wanted to do this."

"She thinks you're my friend," Trevor said in a not very friendly voice. "Friends usually help each other."

"Yeah," Anna said. "And what are you complaining about? You never even did any of the letter."

Logan shrugged his shoulders. "We already went there and told them. How come we needed to say it all over again?"

Trevor didn't feel like arguing. The letter was done. He was glad that part was over too. He was already thinking about something that would be more fun. "I'm going to ask my dad to take us to the Humane Society tonight. Wanna come?"

"Ms. Gilbert said not to make too many plans yet," reminded Anna.

"Oh, Anna, it won't hurt just to look," Kristie said, skipping backwards.

"But Trevor what are you going to do about money?" Anna asked.

"My mom said she'd pay me to wash her delivery van," Trevor told them. "She said my grandpa would have liked a pet if he had been in a seniors' home. And my dad said if I helped with his paper route for a week, he'd give me half his pay."

"Wow," Kristie said. "That's okay!"

"Yeah," Trevor agreed, "except he gets up at 5:30 to do the route."

"Five-thirty in the morning?" shrieked Kristie.

"When it's still dark and spo-o-o-oky," Logan hooted in a deep voice.

Anna bopped him on the head. "Cut it out, Logan. We're not scared you know."

Logan yelled and wailed, pretending to be injured.

"Well we're going to weed my mom's garden," Anna said, "and then Kristie and I are going to collect bottles from all the neighbours along our street."

Trevor waited for Logan to offer an idea. Logan didn't.

But that evening he was there when they all piled

into Trevor's dad's car. It was only a short ride to the Humane Society's animal shelter, but Logan and Kristie argued all the way.

"A white one," Kristie insisted, "with big, floppy ears and..."

"No way!" Logan interrupted. "A white one would get dirty too fast."

Kristie ignored him. "...and long, curly hair."

"It would shed all over the place. Short hair is best."

"Short hair isn't soft enough," Kristie tried to tell him.

"Trevor should get to pick," Anna said. "It was his idea, you know."

"Don't pick a hairy, white one then," Logan joked.

Trevor's dad began to laugh. "Could be the dog will pick you kids," he told them.

A few minutes later, the children knew what he meant. As they moved slowly along an aisle between two rows of kennels, each dog watched them. Some jumped on the gates, trying to be closer to the children. A few barked. Another stood silently wagging its tail. One stayed curled up in a tight ball, its eyes wide open. But one dog seemed to smile at them.

Trevor stopped in front of its kennel. There was something special about this dog. He could feel it. "I think Mr. Granville would like this one."

Logan, Kristie and Anna came to stand beside their friend. The dog they looked at was small, but not too small. It sat looking back, its head tipped to one side. One ear was flopped over, the other stood up stiffly. Its bushy tail slowly swept the floor. It didn't look at all extraordinary.

"What kind is it?" Kristie asked.

Trevor shrugged. "Don't know."

"Right colour," Logan said. "Half grey, half white." He poked Kristie in the ribs with his elbow.

"He has beautiful eyes," Anna crooned.

"Oh yeah, that's important," Logan teased. "Hair's not bad, kinda short but it looks soft."

"Oh Trevor, he's really cute. Do you think he's the one for sure?" asked Kristie.

Trevor didn't speak. The dog's bright black eyes kept him from looking away. He couldn't understand why no one wanted such a dog.

His dad and the girl who worked at the shelter came along then. "Oh, I see you've found Jasper," the girl said. "He's a quiet, friendly fellow."

"Can we let him out?" Trevor asked, still unable to stop staring at the dog.

"Sure. He loves to have visitors."

The gate was opened and Jasper bounded into four pairs of arms. He was soon busy licking hands and faces. His tail wagged non-stop. Finally, he sat down on Trevor's lap and rested his chin on the boy's knee.

"Guess he likes you all right, Trev. He picked you, just like your dad said," Logan remarked.

"Why is Jasper here?" It was what Trevor had been asking himself since the moment he saw the dog. He was so right for Mr. Granville. He knew it. But why didn't the dog already have a home?

"Jasper's owner was very old," the girl explained. "She had to give up her own home and move in with her daughter, but they couldn't take the dog. And Jasper's not a pup, you see. Most people want a younger dog."

"Oh," Kristie gasped. "He'd be perfect for Mr. Granville."

"I wish I could have him," Anna sighed, ruffling Jasper's ears.

Kristie nodded. "Me too."

"My mom's cat wouldn't like him much," Logan mumbled, but Trevor noticed how gently he stroked Jasper.

Trevor hugged the dog close. If he could have a dog, Jasper would be the one. If only his mom didn't have allergies! Instead, he wanted Jasper for Mr. Granville. Jasper was IT!

No one argued on the way home. Hardly a word was spoken. Trevor knew they all had the same thought. Jasper had been at the shelter about 10 days. Dogs were only kept a month. Then they were put to sleep if no one took them home. It didn't seem likely that anyone else would take Jasper. The girl had promised to keep him for three more weeks, since the children wanted him for something so special.

"We can't let Jasper be... killed!" Anna's voice shook as she whispered the last word.

"He won't be. Don't worry. We'll get him out of there." Trevor comforted her with a pat on the back.

"But Trevor, we only have three weeks to get the residents to agree and to get   ¬∩ney," Kristie said. "What if..."

"Don't worry!"

But they did worry all the way home.

Chapter 7

"I think we need $100," Trevor told the girls the next morning. He didn't tell them that would just be the beginning. He hadn't had time to think about how they would keep Jasper fed and everything afterwards. He was glad they didn't ask.

"Wow," Kristie breathed, sitting on the porch step with Anna. "How many pop bottles is that?"

Anna shrugged, and looked worried. "If we each make a share, how much would that be?"

"My dad said $33 each, after we figured out the total last night. Less if we get more people to help." He didn't mention Logan's name.

"But Trevor... $100!" Kristie exclaimed. "They said we could have Jasper for only $20. The other stuff won't cost that much, will it?"

"Want to bet?"

The voice made them jump. No one had seen Logan come up the path. Now he stood there with his hands in his pockets. "There's a licence, that's $10. I checked. A leash and collar is at least $15. We have to get some food, a big bag. And that's not all. The big thing is a trip to the vet. My dad said that might cost $30 or $40!"

Trevor didn't say anything. He was too busy smiling at Logan.

"Gosh!" gasped Kristie. "Why? Jasper's not sick."

"He probably needs shots, and a check-up," Trevor explained to her. "So he won't get sick."

"So, how many pop bottles?" Kristie repeated.

"Lots," Anna moaned. "Lots and lots. More than our whole block has, I bet."

Kristie jumped up from the step. "C'mon then. Let's get my wagon and get going right now."

Logan watched the girls race off, then he turned to Trevor. "Guess I'll go phone my grandma and see if I can wash her car today. What are you going to do?"

Trevor's mouth opened in a big yawn. "I've already done something," he said. "I got up with my dad at 5:30 to deliver papers!"

"Boy! It's a good thing it's only for a week. You'll be dead!"

"But it's for something really important. Right?"

Logan looked his friend right in the eye. "Right!

I'll call you later and tell you how much I've made, okay?"

"Okay. See you."

After Logan left, Trevor counted on his fingers. "Let's see... I'll get $12 after the papers are done. Wonder how I can get some right now?" he thought out loud.

"Hi ho, Hi ho, it's off to work we go," sang Mr. Milton's voice.

Trevor turned to see his dad holding out a garden hoe.

"I'll be at the computer if you need me. Make sure you only take out weeds, okay?" His dad winked at him.

Trevor yawned and reached for the hoe. He felt like sleeping instead. And it was only his first day to get up at 5:30!

Later, Trevor and his dad were eating lunch on the back step when Kristie and Anna came around the side of the house. They dragged a rattley old wagon piled high with bottles and cans.

"Lookit, Trevor. See how many we got?" Kristie was all excited. Anna stood behind her with a big smile on her face.

"How did you get so many?" Trevor wanted to know.

"We told everybody what we were doing it for, so they wouldn't think it was for a ball team or something. People get tired of hearing that, my mom said," Anna explained. "Some gave us extra because they thought

it was such a great idea."

"How many did you get?"

"Thirty-three bottles and 19 cans," Kristie announced proudly. "How much will we make?"

"You can get the calculator from my office," Mr. Milton suggested. Trevor made a fast trip to the basement room that his dad used for his writing.

"You've done well for a start, girls," Mr. Milton said, pushing a few buttons. "Let's see. Thirty-three times 20 cents is $6.60. Five cents each for the cans makes 95 cents. That's $7.55 altogether."

"Oh," said Kristie, suddenly disappointed. "Is that all? I thought it would be more."

"Me too," said Anna.

"Well, it is a good start," Trevor repeated, hoping to cheer them up. "Want me to help you take them to the store?"

Kristie shook her head. "Nope. We'll do it. Maybe we can think of something else to do while we walk. C'mon Anna."

The next day, Logan reported that he'd earned $5 from his grandma. He could go back to the condo again, he said, after his grandma found out if the neighbours wanted their cars done too.

"I could make a fortune doing this," Logan said, as he handed over the money. "Enough to buy some chips and stuff too." When he saw Trevor looking at him, he added, "All this work makes a guy hungry, you know."

Trevor shook his head. Logan would never change.

"Don't eat any of it yet, okay? It's going to be hard to get enough. I only made $4 today. So far we don't even have enough to pay for Jasper."

"This could take forever, you know," Logan groaned.

Trevor sighed. "We don't have that long. You got any more ideas?"

Logan was trying to do a headstand against the tree on Trevor's front lawn. After five tries, he finally stayed upside down. His voice sounded wobbly. "Let's try that bake sale idea someone had. My mom makes great brownies. I bet everybody's mom would make something. And my grandma too."

Trevor smiled. Good old Logan. Always thinking about his stomach. But it might not be a bad idea. And if it took food to keep Logan helping, well, that was fine. "Okay. Let's ask. Maybe we could have it at school."

"Yeah. And how about a garage sale? We could make it just for kids. They'd buy things like old toys you don't use anymore. My mom's always trying to get rid of that stuff. And she's cleaning out the basement this week."

"Boy, maybe standing on your head was a good idea. It made your brain work," Trevor laughed, as he pushed Logan over.

"And it made me hungry," Logan roared, getting to his feet. "Let's go ask Mom for those brownies."

Trevor chased after Logan, who sprinted ahead of him down the street. "Wait up. I'm coming to stop you from eating them all first."

Chapter 8

By the second week, the children had washed more cars, and pulled hundreds of weeds. They had collected cans and bottles from basements and garages. They had even walked dogs for some people. And one neighbour paid Logan to deliver sale flyers for her bookstore. They had a grand total of $54.72. They still had time, but they were running out of ideas.

Trevor asked Ms. Gilbert every day if an answer to their letter had arrived. At last, on Friday, their teacher called them in from the playground before the first bell. There was a white envelope in her hand.

"What does it say?" Kristie hopped up and down, unable to be still another moment.

"I didn't open it yet," Ms. Gilbert said, smiling. "I thought you should." She passed it to Trevor.

The others crowded closer as Trevor clutched the letter tightly. This was it. It had to say yes!

"Hurry up, Trev." Even Logan was excited.

With clumsy fingers, Trevor tore the envelope open. A letter fell out. Kristie bent over to pick it up at the same time as Trevor. They bumped heads.

"Ow!" Kristie exclaimed, rubbing the hurt.

"Sorry," Trevor mumbled, ignoring his own sore head. He unfolded the paper carefully. "It says,

'Dear Trevor and Friends,

I wanted to let you know how the residents felt about your plan to bring a dog to our home. After a long discussion, I'm sorry to say they decided against...'"

Trevor's voice faded away. He couldn't make his eyes move past the word 'against'.

"What does it mean... ? Kristie asked.

"It means no." Trevor spoke quickly but his throat felt tight.

"Oh, how disappointing," Ms. Gilbert said. "It was such a thoughtful plan."

"But why?" Kristie sounded close to tears. "Why don't they want Jasper? He's perfect."

Anna was silent.

Logan scowled darkly. "After all our work! It's not fair!"

Trevor didn't know what to say. He kept hoping he hadn't read the letter correctly. Did it really say the seniors had decided not to accept the offer of a pet? He listened to the reasons, as Ms. Gilbert finished reading the letter. It didn't seem real.

"I was sure the old people would be delighted," Ms. Gilbert said at last. "It seems they just couldn't agree. No one thought Mr. Granville would really want a dog. No one wanted to have to look after it, because they knew he couldn't do it alone."

"Now no one will take Jasper," Anna said in a tiny voice.

They all knew what she meant.

The more Trevor thought about that part, the angrier he got. For the rest of the day he was silent and moody. Even science class, his favourite, was no fun.

By the time school was out, his mind was made up. One way or another, he was going to see that Mr. Granville got a dog. He had to have Jasper. Trevor wanted to see the old man's eyes light up again, like his own grandpa's used to do whenever Trevor had asked for a story about the sea.

He couldn't ask anyone else to help now. It wouldn't be fair, in case he got into trouble. But he would think of something. All he needed was to get a promise from Kristie and Anna and Logan.

43

"Let's not say anything at home yet," Trevor told them after school. He needed time to think. When they looked puzzled, he said, "Then our parents won't be upset too. Okay?"

Kristie's eyes grew big. "You mean, pretend we're still getting Jasper?"

Anna frowned. "It's wrong to tell lies."

"Just don't say anything," Trevor pleaded. "Only for a little while. That isn't the same as telling lies."

Anna looked at Kristie and Logan.

Kristie nodded. "Okay Trevor, we won't," she said. "It's too sad to talk about anyway."

They all looked at Logan, but he just shrugged.

At home, Trevor hunted in the kitchen drawer for the bus schedule. His dad kept it for trips downtown when his mom needed their van at her flower shop. Trevor knew how to choose times and bus numbers from the long list on the card. Now he took a piece of paper and carefully printed the number and times he needed. Then he folded the paper and put it in his pocket. He might need it later, if the plan that was beginning to take shape was going to work.

44

Chapter 9

Trevor felt funny about not telling his mom and dad what the letter had said. But when Mrs. Salatski across the road promised him $10 to paint her picnic table, he kept quiet. A few more jobs like this, and he'd be ready. Too bad it was such a hot day. Sweat trickled down his arm onto the paint brush.

"Trevor! Hey Trevor!" Kristie and Anna skidded their bikes to a stop on the road. "Guess what?"

"What?" Trevor stopped painting and wriggled his stiff fingers.

"We're going to make more money!"

"You don't have to...," he began.

"Anna thinks you're up to something," said Kristie with a sly grin, "and if you are, we still want to help. Don't worry, we won't tell."

Trevor looked at Anna. "What do you mean?"

"My mom saw you out here, painting, when she drove past this morning. She told us 'cause she thinks we're all still earning money for Jasper," Anna explained.

"Are you still thinking of a way to get Jasper, Trevor?" Kristie asked.

Trevor stared at his paint brush. "Maybe," he said. "I can't tell you yet.... I'm not sure."

"That's okay," said Anna. "We just wanted to tell you we're going to set up a lemonade stand. It's so hot out, lots of people will buy it." She pulled Kristie's arm. "We're on our way to the store for lemonade." The girls waved and peddled off.

Maybe things were looking up again. Trevor sighed. It might work. A few more days. A few more dollars. It might still work. He picked up his paint brush and let a small pale blue pool drip onto the table top. Two smaller drips became ears, and he added a streak for a tail. Legs completed his picture of Jasper, before he slowly spread out the paint.

After supper, Logan came over. "Want to play some football over at my house?"

"Nah. Too tired. Got to get up early to do papers," Trevor said resting his head against the porch railing.

"How come you're still working all the time? The letter said no, remember?" Logan scratched a mosquito bite on his arm. A small red blob oozed out. "Hey, maybe you could sell blood to the Red Cross!"

Trevor made a face. "Get real, Logan. They don't buy it. Especially from kids. We probably don't even have enough to give away."

"Well it doesn't matter anyway. C'mon and play instead."

Trevor shook his head. Playing could wait. He looked over at the van parked in their driveway.

"Wish I was big enough to drive. I could deliver the flowers from my mom's shop," he said, sighing.

"If you were that big, you could buy Jasper for yourself since those people at the home don't want him," Logan said. "Hey, Trevor how long are you going to keep that letter a big secret...?" He stopped when he saw the look on Trevor's face.

Trevor knew Logan hadn't noticed the creak of the screen door behind him. But he knew his dad had heard every word. He bit his lip.

It was a good thing Logan left right away. Trevor felt like screaming at him. Instead, he had to tell his mom and dad about the letter. He knew they were disappointed in him, even though they were sorry that the plan had failed. His mom told him to think of another way to do something for the seniors.

In bed later, Trevor couldn't sleep. He tossed until the covers were a tangled mess. Logan had spoiled everything. It was Logan's fault that he'd have to stop raising money. Logan hadn't even wanted to help in the first place. Logan was supposed to be his best friend.

It felt rotten when your best friend let you down. How could Trevor let Mr. Granville down? And Jasper needed a home — right away. If he didn't get the dog soon... Trevor couldn't bear to think about it.

He crept out of bed and over to his desk. He opened the drawer slowly so his parents wouldn't hear. The piece of paper with the bus times was still where he'd left it. Good! He'd need it now. It was up to him to keep his promise, no matter what!

At 4:00 the next afternoon, Trevor got off the bus one block from the animal shelter. In his pocket was enough money for Jasper, and bus fare to the seniors' home. The girl at the desk remembered him.

"Hi. Didn't your dad come with you?"

"N..no. He's meeting me here in a few minutes." Trevor hated having to lie, but he didn't know if the girl would let him take Jasper by himself.

"Well, I need him to sign the papers for the dog," the girl explained.

Oh no. Trevor hadn't thought about anything like that. His mind raced. What could he say? His knees began to shake.

"Um, he'll be here in a while. I brought the money. Can I wait outside with Jasper?" It might work. He might have to stand around for a few minutes, in case she was watching. But not for too long. He didn't want to miss the bus. If he could just wander down to the corner, he'd be out of sight.

"I guess so," the girl said. "I'll get the dog for you. Do you have a leash?"

Trevor nodded. Thank goodness he'd remembered to bring a piece of rope. "We haven't finished collecting the money for a real leash and stuff yet," he told the girl, as he pulled some crumpled bills from his pocket. "But we wanted to be sure to get Jasper."

The girl was busy writing on a paper. She didn't seem interested in Trevor's story. He was getting hot, and his mouth had gone dry. He hoped she didn't ask any more questions.

Jasper greeted Trevor with wiggles and licks. He didn't bark, which was good. Trevor wanted him to be quiet on the bus. He picked the dog up, and turned to leave. "My dad will be along," he said over his shoulder.

A car had pulled up in front. Two people got out. They would keep the girl busy for a few minutes. It was all the time he needed. He took off around the corner, expecting to hear the girl calling after him.

Chapter 10

"We don't allow dogs on the bus, Sonny." the bus driver said as Trevor stepped up to pay his money.

Trevor's heart almost stopped. Why hadn't he thought about this either?

He looked down the aisle, and saw only four people on the bus. "I'm just taking him to visit my grandpa. At the seniors' home on Spring Street." It was the first thing that popped into his head. Trevor didn't think that counted as a lie.

The driver glanced in the rear-view mirror. "Well, that's only a few stops, and I haven't got time to argue this time." He pointed to the dog. "But you keep him still."

Trevor nodded and scurried to a seat near the back of the bus where he thought the driver couldn't see

him. He clutched Jasper firmly on his lap. When a police car came alongside the bus, he froze. But the car sped off.

He hadn't exactly stolen the dog. The money had been paid. And if his plan worked, his dad would go to sign the paper. Later. That hadn't exactly been a lie either. He just hadn't said how much later. He knew his mom and dad would be mad, but he hoped they would understand.

"I've got to take you to your new home, Jasper," he whispered urgently into the dog's upright ear.

Jasper swished his tail across Trevor's knee. He was looking eagerly out the window as the bus moved down the street.

"You'll like it there, I know you will," Trevor continued. "Mr. Granville will love you. I can hardly wait to see his face. And I'll come and visit a lot to take you for walks, okay?"

Trevor was positive the residents would change their minds once they saw Mr. Granville and Jasper together. They'd have to keep Jasper. He was so sure, he didn't even stop to wonder what he would do with the dog if his plan didn't work.

Jasper was starting to wriggle by the time the bus reached the seniors' home. Trevor was glad to get off before the driver said anything. He led the dog around the building to the window where Mr. Granville always sat.

Mr. Granville wasn't there.

Trevor stared at the window, unbelieving. The old man was always there. Now what?

Looking around, he saw a park bench by a tree. He tied Jasper's rope to the leg of the bench with a tight knot.

"You stay here. And don't fuss. Maybe no one will see you. I've got to find out where Mr. Granville is. Be good." He patted Jasper on the head and turned away.

Jasper barked.

"Sh-sh-sh! Don't do that. I'll be right back."

Jasper sat down, put his head on one side, and whined.

Trevor frowned. If the dog was noisy, someone might come to check. He tried again. "Stay," he said firmly. "Quiet."

This time Jasper was silent. Trevor hoped it would last. He went in the front door, and looked around. The whole place was quiet. Then a door opened along the hall, and a young woman came toward him.

"Hi. Looking for someone, Dear?"

"Mr. Granville. I came to see Mr. Granville. Do you know where he is?"

The woman looked at her watch. "He must be in his room. Probably having a nap."

Oh great, Trevor thought. "What time does he get up?" It was getting late. His mother had told him to go and make up with Logan, but if he wasn't home by suppertime, she'd call and find out he hadn't been there. Then he'd be in double trouble.

"Soon, I think. But it isn't really the best time to visit. Could you come back?"

Trevor shook his head, his eyes growing wide. Good grief, how could he come back? What would he do with Jasper? "I have to show him something, that's all," he tried.

"Well, let me see if he's up then," the woman said, smiling.

"Could you bring him to that window?" Trevor said, pointing.

"Yes, I guess so." Now the woman sounded puzzled.

Trevor waited by the front door, too impatient to stand still. At last, he saw Mr. Granville in his wheelchair being steered down the hall. He ran outside. By the time he had Jasper untied, the old man was in his usual place at the window.

Trevor waved, and pointed to the dog. He clapped his hands so Jasper would jump up and down. Then he pretended to run away, so Jasper would chase him. At last, he rolled on the grass and the dog jumped all over him. Pretty soon, Trevor was out of breath. Jasper, at least, was having fun!

But when Trevor looked up to see what Mr. Granville was doing, no one was there.

"Oh no!" Trevor wailed. "He wasn't there long enough to see. What happened?"

Without thinking, he raced back to the front door, Jasper in tow. Inside, they almost collided with Mrs. Spencer, the Director. She was taking Mr. Granville back down the hall.

"Young man! Stop right there." she began angrily. "This is not a playground." She stopped, and looked more closely at Trevor. "Oh, you're the boy who wanted to get the dog. And this, I presume, is the dog."

Trevor was frozen to the spot. Everything was going wrong.

"But, Dear, didn't you understand? We decided not to have a pet."

"I know. Yes, we got the letter," Trevor began. "But I thought if..."

Suddenly Mr. Granville made a strange noise. Trevor and Mrs. Spencer looked around. Jasper was standing in front of the wheelchair, his paws up on the old man's knees, his tail waving happily. Mr. Granville was smiling, rubbing the dog's head, and trying to talk to him.

"My word!" Mrs. Spencer declared. "That's amazing. I never imagined..." She looked at Trevor. "Can you stay a bit longer? I think the rest of the folks here need to see this!"

Chapter 11

Trevor felt dizzy. He nodded, then shook his head, then nodded again. "I mean, my mom, she's expecting me for supper."

"We'll phone. Come with me." Mrs. Spencer led the way to her office pushing Mr. Granville with Jasper trotting along behind.

Trevor listened nervously as Mrs. Spencer talked to his mother on the phone. He felt his face grow hot when she said, "Oh, I see. He didn't tell you?"

Trevor looked over at Mr. Granville, with Jasper now curled up contentedly on his knee. It was exactly the way he had pictured it. It would all be worth it, he felt, as long as Jasper got to stay. He squeezed both hands together in his lap. He'd explain how he had

to do it. He wished the other kids could see the old man and the dog together.

At last Mrs. Spencer hung up. "Was my mom mad?" Trevor asked, even though he already knew the answer.

Mrs. Spencer sighed. "Well young man, it seems you will have some explaining to do. But your mother told me how hard you children have worked. She's coming to pick you up. Now we'd better get everyone together and see what we can do about this dog, hadn't we?"

Trevor ran to push Mr. Granville's chair. With Mrs. Spencer on their side, he was sure everything would be all right. If only there was time to call Anna and Kristie.

While the residents gathered in the big room, Trevor stayed close to Mr. Granville's side. The old man kept one hand on Trevor's arm while he scratched Jasper's floppy ear with the other.

Mrs. Murphy came over right away. "Isn't he a wonderful dog, everyone?" she said. "And look at Thomas!" She pointed to Mr. Granville. "Look how thrilled he is. You are such a thoughtful boy," she whispered to Trevor. "I voted for your plan, you know. But some of the others couldn't see it working. They'll change their minds now, you'll see."

Another friend, Trevor thought happily. He'd need all he could get in the next few minutes.

"This is the boy who came up with the idea for a pet," Mrs. Spencer began. "It seems he doesn't want to take no for an answer. And this is Jasper," she said, while Jasper perked up his ears and wagged his tail at the sound of his name. "What do you think?" Mrs. Spencer asked them all. "Shall we have this dog for Thomas?"

Trevor held his breath.

"Who's going to take it out for walks?" a tall, thin man grumbled. "Thomas can't and a dog needs walks. I did enough dog walking in the pouring rain in my day."

"I'll walk Jasper for you," Trevor said eagerly. "And some of my friends will help too."

"Now that I see him, he's not as big as I thought he might be," said a lady in a green sweatsuit. "I think I might enjoy a short walk now and then."

Several others nodded.

"Does he have fleas?" another lady asked. "They're so hard to get rid of."

Trevor opened his mouth to say what he thought of that remark, but Mrs. Murphy stopped him. "My daughter-in-law has a dog-grooming business. I'm sure she'd give Jasper a regular check-up."

Trevor smiled gratefully.

A few people were worried about noise, but Jasper hadn't made a sound so far. Trevor told them how quiet Jasper had been on the bus. Someone else asked who would pay for his food. Trevor explained how he planned to offer part of his allowance, if they'd let him visit Jasper often.

But it was Mr. Granville who really saved the day. He seemed to be more alert now. Trevor realized the old man was looking at the other residents who had gathered around to pet the dog. But he kept one hand on Trevor and the other on Jasper. And the strange sound he made, Trevor knew, was laughter.

When Mrs. Spencer called for a vote, all but three of the residents raised their hands. Those who voted yes turned to see who hadn't, and soon those three hands slowly went up too.

Trevor wanted to cheer out loud. Behind him, someone did. He turned to see his mom standing at the door - and beside her was Logan.

Trevor started to frown, but then he saw the look on his mom's face. Her hand rested on Logan's shoulder. All at once he was glad to see his best friend again. Logan may have made him mad, but because of it, Jasper was here today. And now everything was going to work out.

"Jasper looked like he belonged there, all right," Trevor said, as he and Logan finished telling the tale to Anna and Kristie.

"I wish we could have seen them. When can we go and visit, Trevor?" Anna asked.

"Any day, after school. I told them one of us would walk Jasper," Trevor explained. He looked at them both. "You will help, won't you?"

"We can take turns," Kristie announced. "But Trevor, weren't your mom and dad mad?" she asked, her eyes wide.

"Yeah. Didn't you get grounded?" Anna wondered.

"Grounded might have been better," Logan said in his headstand voice. "Tell 'em, Trevor."

Trevor yawned and rolled over onto his stomach on the lawn. "I got sentenced - to two more weeks of delivering papers. Starting tomorrow!"

"At 5:30?" Anna gasped.

"Yup. But it's okay. Logan promised to help, for an extra breakfast. And it means Jasper can stay!"

But the best part, Trevor thought, is now I've got a new grandpa to visit!

ABOUT THE AUTHOR

GILLIAN RICHARDSON lives in Salmon Arm, B.C. In addition to writing novels, short stories and magazine articles, she is an elementary school teacher-librarian. Her novels for children include *One Chance to Win* (Ragweed 1986), which was a Canadian Children's Book Centre "Our Choice" selection and *The Migration of Robyn Birchwood* (Nimbus 1991). She is also the author of *Saskatchewan* (Lerner 1995). Gillian received a Saskatchewan Writers' Guild (SWG) literary award for children's literature for *Great Goose Round-up* in 1995 and an honorable mention in 1996 for *On Wings of Hope*.

ABOUT THE ILLUSTRATOR

CLAUDETTE MACLEAN is a new-media visual communications specialist. Through her freelance graphic design and illustration business, she provides advertising and promotions services for corporate clients using traditional media, multi-media and the web. Claudette also takes on portrait commissions and her favourite subjects are children. She, her husband Brian, sons Scott and Sean, and their dog Patch, live in Edmonton.

A teacher's guide for A Friend for Mr. Granville is available from Hodgepog Books.